Netball Dreams

hardie grant EGMONT

Netball Dreams
first published in 2007
this edition published in 2013 by
Hardie Grant Egmont
Ground Floor, Building 1, 658 Church Street
Richmond, Victoria 3121, Australia
www.hardiegrantegmont.com.au

A CiP record for this title is available from the National Library of Australia

Text copyright © 2007 Thalia Kalkipsakis
Illustration and design copyright © 2013 Hardie Grant Egmont

Illustration by Aki Fukuoka
Design by Michelle Mackintosh
Text design and typesetting by Ektavo

Printed in Australia by Griffin Press, an Accredited ISO AS/NZS
14001:2004 Environmental Management System printer.

3 5 7 9 10 8 6 4 2

FSC
www.fsc.org
MIX
Paper from
responsible sources
FSC® C009448

The paper this book is printed on is certified against the
Forest Stewardship Council® Standards. Griffin Press holds
FSC chain of custody certification SGS-COC-005088. FSC
promotes environmentally responsible, socially beneficial
and economically viable management of the world's forests

Netball Dreams

by
Thalia Kalkipsakis

Illustrations by
Aki Fukuoka

hardie grant EGMONT

Chapter One

I held my breath and crossed my fingers. Inside my runners, I tried to cross my toes. But there wasn't enough room for that.

Pick me, pick me, pick me, I said over and over in my head.

I was standing on our school netball courts in the cool winter sun. Around me was a crowd of kids. So I didn't like my chances of being picked soon. Two classes is a lot of kids to choose from.

Callum was standing out the front with the five other team captains, deciding who to pick for his team.

'Hey, Alex,' whispered Becky beside me. 'Hope we're on Callum's team.'

Becky's my best friend in the whole world. Sometimes – like now – she can even read my mind.

'Of course he'll choose you!' I said, and made a sloppy kissing sound.

Callum and Becky have known each other forever. They almost kissed once!

I knew Callum would choose Becky. He had already chosen his best friends, Mickey and Brad. That was why I was crossing my fingers – I wanted to stay with Becky. I didn't want to be left out!

Becky just rolled her eyes at my kissing sound. She seemed calm.

But I wasn't calm. I could feel my peanut butter sandwich churning around in my stomach.

The teams being chosen now were for a whole term of netball. If I made it onto a team with Becky and the gang, it would be a term of jokes and fun. But if I didn't get picked with my friends, there was no telling what might happen.

Now it was Callum's third pick. Becky stood straight and hopeful next to me.

'Um … Becky,' said Callum.

When she heard her name, Becky did a little jump and clapped her hands. Her blonde plaits bounced on her shoulders.

'Don't worry,' Becky said, and winked. Then she headed out the front to stand with Callum, Mickey and Brad.

Now I was on my own. And I *was* worried. Callum was good friends with Becky. But he was only friends with me *because* of Becky.

Will he choose me for his team?

He wasn't going to choose me for my netball skills, that's for sure. In fact, no-one was going to choose me for my netball skills. Balls and me? We don't really mix.

If I try to throw a ball somewhere, it's more likely to end up anywhere except where I want it to go. Around me, balls have a mind of their own.

And catching them? Let's just say, it's really hard to catch a ball with your eyes squeezed shut. So I was going to be left until the end — with all the kids that no-one wants on their team. Whoever got stuck with me would spend all term wishing that I wasn't on their team. And I was going to spend all term wishing the same thing.

Callum's team was my only hope.

Chapter Two

Soon my peanut butter sandwich felt like wobbly mush in my stomach. I wasn't standing in the middle of a crowd anymore. Most kids had already been picked for a team.

I was standing in a row with about ten other left-overs. None of us were any good at sport.

The captains were scratching their heads and frowning. It felt pretty bad, as if we had a sign over our heads, saying WE CAN'T PLAY NETBALL.

Callum had chosen two more people after Becky – Angie and Claire. Angie and Claire were both on Callum's basketball team. We call them the Basketball Girls. They're tall and good at sport. It made sense that he picked them.

Now was the last chance for Callum to pick me. I held my breath.

Then I heard it. The word I wanted so much to hear. 'Alex!'

When Callum called my name, he laughed, as if he had been planning to choose me all along. Maybe he *did* count me as a friend. With a cheer, I ran up and hugged Becky. Angie and Claire did a high five.

'This team is going to be so awesome!' said Claire.

I'm so glad I'm not a left-over!

It felt good to escape the left-overs, but I felt sorry for them, too.

Tony, a boy in the other class, was the last one left. Tony's really bad at sport. Even worse than me. And that's saying something!

When he was finally picked, Tony did a silly cheer with both arms in the air. But I knew that inside he must have felt bad.

Then Mr Dwyer clapped his hands. He's our P.E. teacher and he's pretty cool. He calls me 'Awesome Alex', even though I'm not awesome at sport. Mr Dwyer is nice to everyone.

'All right, people!' called Mr Dwyer, clapping his hands again to get our attention.

'Take a seat while I explain what's going to happen.'

There was shuffling and chatting as everyone sat. The ground felt rough and hard under my legs. But I didn't mind. All I could think about was how glad I was to be on a team with my friends.

'The netball tournament starts in two weeks,' called Mr Dwyer.

Callum gave us all a thumbs-up, as if he was expecting us to win.

'Next week, I want you to get to know your team,' continued Mr Dwyer. He paced in front of us like an army captain in front of his troops. 'Some team members have good ball skills and lots of experience.

Others have less experience,' he added.

I didn't look at Mr Dwyer when he said that. I knew he was talking about people like me.

'But *everyone* brings something special to their team,' called Mr Dwyer, and punched his fist in the air. 'I want you all to remember that.'

I brushed an ant off my leg. *Everyone brings something special?* Around balls, nothing I did was special.

But at least, when I did nothing special this term, I would be doing it with my friends.

Chapter Three

'I'm out the back!' called Mum, when she heard me get home from school.

I pinched two rice balls from the fridge. Then I went out the back door to see Mum. The rich smell of fresh soil met me. I had to step carefully to keep my shoes clean.

'How was school?' asked Mum.

She shook dirt from a bunch of carrots

and dropped them in a basket.

'Good,' I said, as I munched on a rice ball. 'I'm on a netball team with Becky and the gang.'

Mum wiped a strand of hair from her forehead and left a smudge of dirt. 'Really! That's like basketball, is it?'

Mum's about as sporty as I am. She hardly knows anything about sport. I kept eating the rice balls as I explained the difference between basketball and netball. Mr Dwyer had taught us that already.

'And that's why the best players are Angie, Claire and Callum,' I finished.

Mum came to stand near me. She looked at me with a faraway look in her eye. Then she cupped my face in her hands, like she was holding a baby. 'You'll be great on a team, Alex,' Mum said, smiling. 'You're good with people.'

I let Mum kiss my forehead. Then I headed back inside feeling happy. Maybe I could do something special on the team, after all.

The next week in P.E. class, all six teams stood in groups around the netball courts. It was time to decide who would play in each position.

In netball, each player has a specific job

to do — like shooting goals, or stopping the other team from getting goals.

I didn't think I would be good in *any* position. Unless 'score keeper' was one.

Callum turned to face us. He clapped his hands like Mr Dwyer always does. 'Right,' he said. 'I'm playing centre, and let's see …'

He scratched his head as he continued. 'Mickey's goal shooter, and Brad is goal defence – '

But he didn't get any further through the positions than that.

'Hang on!' Angie said, her arms crossed. 'You're not the boss, Callum.'

'Yes I am. I'm captain,' he said, standing tall and proud.

Mickey did a joke salute, like he was in the army. Brad laughed, but Claire and Becky scowled with Angie.

'We're meant to work this out together,' said Angie. Her dark eyes were flashing. It didn't look like she was going to be bossed around by Callum.

I like Angie. She's strong, and nice. But I didn't want her to start a fight. So I decided to speak up.

'Well, why don't we make Angie vice-captain?' I suggested.

The whole team looked at me. A netball flew past. But no-one moved. There was complete silence while everyone thought about my idea.

'You both know heaps about sport,' I said. 'But this way, you can work together so no-one is the boss!'

Angie's eyes shone. Callum was nodding, as if he liked the idea. I sneaked a glance at Becky. I wasn't sure if she'd feel jealous of Angie being vice-captain, with Callum as captain.

But Becky was beaming. She looked proud of my idea. Before long, Callum and Angie had decided all the positions together – without any fighting.

They picked me for wing defence. That was fine with me. From what I could tell, playing wing defence meant I had to run after the wing attack from the other team. And when they caught the ball I had to flap my arms a lot and try to stop them throwing it where they wanted.

Maybe all that flapping was why they called it wing *defence?* Well, the idea gave me a giggle.

'OK, let's get to work,' said Callum.

He pulled a netball from a sack at the edge of the netball courts. Then he started spinning it on his finger like a basketball.

My heart sank. A ball. I always look like an idiot around balls. *Am I about to look silly in front of my friends?*

Chapter Four

That first day of training, the netball really had a mind of it own. It was like a cheeky little gremlin.

Each time I touched it, the ball would fly off the court, or go crazy and crooked. So annoying! But, to my relief, everyone was super nice to me.

If I dropped the ball, someone would call out, 'Never mind.' And if I threw the ball crooked, someone else would call, 'Good try, Alex.' They didn't make me feel bad at all.

Once I even managed a solid catch, followed by a not-bad pass to Becky. When I did that, the whole gang clapped and cheered. Anyone watching would've thought I'd actually done something useful!

It was brilliant seeing the sporty kids in action. The Basketball Girls were so cool to watch. One of them would throw the ball to no-one – just a gap. And I would think, *hey, I'm not so bad. Other people throw the ball dumb places, too.*

But somehow the other one would charge into the gap. Like magic, she would always be there to catch the ball!

The first time they did it, I thought it was just a fluke.

But they kept doing it. Over and over. Even Callum and Mickey managed to do it sometimes.

Those kids really know a lot about throwing and catching balls.

By the time P.E. was over for the day, I realised something amazing. Even though I was still clumsy and awkward, it felt great to be part of a team. For the first time ever, I started to see what the sporty kids liked about sport.

I even started looking forward to the tournament. It was going to be fun playing a real game with my team.

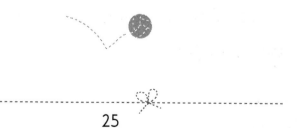

Tooooot! Mr Dwyer blew the whistle and shook his head at Angie.

She made a face and said 'Drat!' under her breath.

'Never mind,' Callum called to Angie. But he didn't look happy.

This was our first game for the tournament. And it wasn't going well. Everything seemed to be going wrong. Angie and Claire had heaps of shots at the goal. But the ball hardly ever went in.

Sometimes the ball would fly over the ring, as if aiming for a backboard that wasn't there. Other times, one of us would break a rule, so the ball would be given to the other team.

Not good at all.

Of course, I was doing nothing special as I had expected.

At first I thought that defence would be easy. Just a lot of arm-flapping and getting in the way. But good defenders actually

stop the other team scoring. And really good defenders even steal the ball and get it to their own attackers.

I knew all that by watching the other team. They were great. They kept stealing the ball from us and getting it to their shooter, super fast. Again and again.

By half-time, we were ten goals behind. Our team stood in a huddle with red faces and drooping mouths. No-one was enjoying losing.

'I wish we were playing basketball,' said Claire, frowning.

Callum nodded glumly.

'Yeah, netball's so — ' Angie started to say.

But she didn't get any further, because I butted in. Claire had given me an idea.

Chapter Five

'What if we *were* playing basketball?' I said quickly.

The half-time break wasn't very long. If we were going to play better, we had to think of something fast.

'That's the problem!' groaned Callum.

'But you don't always win at basketball, do you?' I said, my hands on my hips.

'What happens when you're *losing* a game of basketball?'

Callum's and Angie's eyes met. I could see new ideas forming in their minds.

'Well, our coach would make some changes,' said Angie.

She and Callum started talking quickly, their heads together, arms gesturing.

After a while, they turned to the rest of the team with a new plan. Callum and Angie swapped some of our players around – Angie as centre, and Callum on defence with Mickey and me.

Angie turned to me and smiled. 'Alex,' she said, 'stick to your player like glue.'

I nodded. Then Callum called to the team, 'OK, let's do it!'

'YEAH!' we all cried, and raced onto the court. We were pumped and keen to win.

My player moved fast. My throat was dry from puffing. My cheeks were burning hot. But nothing could shake me off her. I was like superglue. Wherever she went, I went too.

The changes Angie and Callum had made to our positions were working, and our team's hope seemed to lift. Before I knew it, Claire had scored. Our team cheered as if we had won. Because now we thought we *could* win.

Again we scored. And again. Suddenly it almost seemed easy. By three-quarter time, we were only six goals behind. The gap was closing.

Soon we were only five goals down.

With only a minute to go, we were two goals down. We had a chance to win!

But the other team had the ball. They were about to score. Up went the ball, hovering on the side of the ring. But it didn't fall in.

It fell off the ring, straight into Callum's hands. Our team cheered!

I'm not sure what happened then. My player was running, trying to dodge me. I was being superglue. As my player ran into a gap, I heard Callum calling my name. 'Aleeeeex!'

This was it! The ball was flying towards me. I gulped and tried not to close my eyes. A thought flashed through my head.

I have to catch this. I have to —

But the ball didn't touch my fingers.

Like a cat leaping at a toy, my player plucked the ball from the air. I gasped — not just from surprise, but also because of what it meant.

The ball, the game, everything was suddenly out of my hands.

Before I knew it, the ball was falling through the other team's goal. *Oh no. That was my fault.*

With wide eyes I stared at Callum. Would he yell at me for losing the ball? Or worse, would he wish I wasn't on the team?

But Callum was already running back to his starting position. 'Never mind, Alex,' he called.

Behind me Becky called out, 'Good try, Alex.'

No-one seemed to blame me for losing the ball. I kept my head down and kept playing. The rest of the team were acting as if we could still win. But there was no time to catch up.

Our chance to win was gone.

Chapter Six

Mmmm ... crunchy, salty, munchy, yummy peanut butter.

The day after our first game, I sat on the office steps with the rest of the team, thinking about peanut butter.

I eat crunchy peanut butter sandwiches for lunch every day. The only thing I like to change is the bread – white, multigrain.

My favourite is rye. That was what I was eating that day.

I was thinking a whole heap about peanut butter. But I wasn't saying much. No-one was. Everyone was quiet and glum, disappointed about losing our first game of netball.

Even Angie and Claire were sitting with us instead of playing basketball. For once, there was another game that they cared about more.

I scrunched up the cling wrap from my sandwich and threw it down the office steps. I was aiming for a rubbish bin at the bottom. But just like a gremlin ball, the cling wrap didn't do what I wanted.

It curved up, seemed to float in the air for a second, then fell silently onto the bottom step. Why did I even bother!

'Good try, Alex,' said Becky with a small smile.

Dunk ... plop. Callum threw his empty drink box at the recycling bin. But it didn't go in either. It bounced off the side and lay at the bottom of the steps. He sighed.

Callum was taking our loss yesterday pretty hard.

Normally I don't care about losing at sport. I'm used to it! But I felt bad about losing the ball yesterday because I'd let the team down. I know how hard everyone had tried to win.

By now, Angie had finished her lunch. She threw her paper bag at the bin. It sailed in with perfect aim. 'Woo hoo,' said Angie. But her voice sounded flat.

I glanced past Claire at Angie's sad face. *Poor Angie. Poor team!*

How could I cheer up my friends? I jumped down the steps and put my cling wrap and Callum's drink box in the bin.

'We need a name!' I said from the bottom of the steps. I didn't have to say *for our netball team*. Everyone knew straight away what I was talking about.

'Yeah!' said everyone. In a row, the team sat a little straighter.

'The Cockatoos?' asked Claire.

No-one liked that idea much. That name was already taken for their basketball team. But we had other ideas. Already the glum mood was gone.

'The Kookaburras?'

'The Rosellas?'

'The Mean Team!'

That last idea came from Mickey. When he said it, he jumped up and did a face like an angry wrestler. He's such a boy.

But I liked how his idea rhymed. And then I thought of it – the perfect name for our team.

'The Dream Team!' I cried. 'Like … we're all friends. So we really are the perfect team.'

Angie and Claire did a high five. Then Becky joined in. Even the boys seemed happy with our new name.

We started talking then, loud and excited, about what went wrong yesterday and how we could play better. We talked and planned right until the end of lunch.

Ding, ding, ding . . .

When the bell rang, we walked down the steps together and headed for class.

The other kids scattered, running in different directions and doing their own thing.

But we stayed together. We walked as a group, talking and laughing like a gang. The Dream Team, together.

Chapter Seven

Now we had a name. We started hanging out all the time after that. Even when we weren't playing netball, we sat and talked as a team.

Angie and Claire stopped playing basketball at lunchtime. Amazing! Of course, most of the time we played netball anyway. It was fun. When the lunch bell rang, we would gulp down our food, eager to be first down at the courts.

The rest of the team were getting better and better, learning not to step or bounce the ball. They were shooting better, too.

Angie spent heaps of time with me. She was my sporty superhero.

Sometimes we just played catch. Slow at first, then faster and faster until I was

throwing with force. Soon I learnt to catch a fast ball, like catching a giant bullet.

'Aim at the bib,' Angie would say. 'Not the person's face.' And sometimes I did just that.

Becky and I made a poster on my dad's computer. Before each netball game, we would tie it to the fence.

Then we would stand in a circle and pile our hands in the middle, one on top of the other until we couldn't tell whose hand was whose. Together, we would throw up our hands and call out, 'Go, Dream Team!' It was brilliant. Doing that made my whole body buzz, ready to play the game.

We lost our next game. The other team had four girls who played on a real team after school. Those girls were really competitive and played like bull terriers — angry and unstoppable.

We only lost by three goals, so we didn't feel too bad. It's not all about winning, after all.

Then, for our third game, I had my first taste of victory. Suddenly, I understood why the others tried so hard to win.

Whoops!

Someone dropped the ball. But it wasn't me. It was Tony, the boy who was last to be picked. We were playing against his team.

Quickly I reached down, fumbling for the rolling ball. Tony didn't even try to stop me. Then I had it. Solid in my hands.

I'd better make this pass.

'Here, Alex!' called Becky.

With good aim for once, I passed the ball to her.

'Sorry,' mumbled Tony. But his team didn't say 'never mind'. They didn't say anything. I was glad that I didn't get stuck on that team!

Over, across, and up went the ball, as it was passed and shot through our goal. Another goal for us! And we were already winning.

With each point and each pass of the ball, our team moved closer to something exciting, just around the corner. It was like finally making it to Christmas Eve.

Near the end of the game, I saw a

little smile on Angie's face. Even Callum stopped frowning. Then, at last, the final whistle blew.

Like pins attracted to a magnet, we rushed together, jumping up and down, hugging and doing high fives.

It was brilliant. I was light and happy and proud, high on the taste of a win. It was such an amazing feeling, being part of the winning team. I wanted to feel that way again.

Chapter Eight

All week after our win, I wanted to celebrate! Becky and I made up a chant.

Dream Team are the win-ners!

Dream Team are the win-ners!

As we sang we did a silly dance, kicking our legs out to the side. We did it all recess, until some of the other kids called, 'The Dream Team stinks!' But we just laughed.

Winning with the Dream Team made me feel bold and strong and part of something important.

We won our fourth game by three points. It wasn't easy, though. Sometimes the ball moved so fast I didn't know what was happening.

But it was an important win, because now we had a chance at the grand final. Imagine that! If we won our fifth game, we would qualify for it. I had never been in a grand final. But I was sure it would be fun.

The week before our fifth game, we practised whenever we could. The whole team was hungry to win.

And at the start of the next game, we were pumped. It was as if we were zapped with electricity. We had springs in our legs and suction caps on our hands.

Soon the ball was flying. *Zig, zag, zap!* It moved through our hands with speed.

Just before half-time, the scores were level. Angie was playing centre. She was blazing across the court like a bushfire. I could tell she wanted to get ahead before half-time.

She had the ball and was trying to get it to our attackers. But the other team were good defenders. They weren't making it easy for Angie.

Forward went the ball. Then it would hit a dead end, the other team blocking our players. Back came the ball to Angie.

Suddenly, Angie seemed to change her mind. She threw the ball to Becky. Then Angie ran backwards, calling for the ball again. I kept my eye on Angie and stayed with my player. But I wasn't sure what was going on.

What was Angie doing? She was running *away* from our goal.

Becky threw Angie the ball. And before I knew it, Angie was calling my name.

'Aleeeex!'

I ran closer, to clear my player. *Flash* came the ball, rushing towards me.

I reached my hands up, eyes on the ball. But it came faster than I was expecting. Faster than ever before.

My fingers touched the ball. But I wasn't ready for the blazing speed of it. The ball kept flying. It slipped through my fingers.

Whack!

Like a sudden punch the ball hit me straight in the face.

Chapter Nine

I don't like seeing my own blood. No-one does. But I saw a lot of it that day and it was gross.

After I was hit in the face, blood started pouring out of my nose. Some of it splattered on the netball court, leaving a dirty red stain. But most of it splattered onto my top.

The whole team crowded around me, with Mr Dwyer telling them all to move back. I could hear Angie next to me, almost sobbing. 'Sorry! Gosh, I'm so sorry, Alex.'

Mr Dwyer sat me on the bench with a big blue ice-pack on my nose. Not very attractive! My nose wasn't broken, it was just bleeding from being hit so hard.

I felt terrible. Not because of the pain. That stopped. And not because of the blood, either. I felt terrible because of that gremlin ball. Why, why, *why* hadn't I caught it?

Angie had spent so much time practising with me. But when it really mattered, I still couldn't catch the ball.

Mr Dwyer clapped his hands and looked

at Callum. 'You folks will have to play on with six players,' he said.

Callum nodded and shrugged. But I couldn't look anyone in the eye.

Six players. Not good at all.

Everyone else ran back onto the court to finish the game.

I sat like a sack of potatoes, feeling glum and full of doom. I knew what was going to happen. The Dream Team was going to lose this game, and lose our chance at the grand final.

And all because I couldn't catch a ball.

When everyone started playing again, something amazing happened. Our team got the first goal.

It was only a short time into the second half. And we were already ahead! I moved the ice-pack a bit, so I could see better.

Angie was amazing, racing here and dashing there. And all the others played so hard that soon their faces were glowing red and their hairlines were sweaty. But it was working.

Our team was winning.

I sat on the bench, peering past the ice-pack, watching our score creep up.

I hope our team can win.

Three goals ahead. Then four …

A strange, sad feeling came over me. It didn't matter that I wasn't playing – my team was winning without me.

The strange feeling grew stronger. I started thinking back to the start of term and how I was picked last on the team.

In our first game I had lost the ball to the other team. Our team lost that game *because of me*. Slowly I went though all our games and all my mistakes. *A hundred mistakes with the gremlin ball.*

I didn't care about my nose anymore. I pulled off the ice-pack and dropped it on the bench. I felt all mixed up as I sat there, looking like Rudolf the red-nosed reindeer, watching my team's score go up and up.

When they won the game, I clapped from the side while the team jumped and cheered out on the court. We were in the grand final.

But inside I felt kind of sad and left-out. Worried questions flashed through my mind.

What if I had kept playing today? Would I have made more mistakes and stopped my team from winning?

Maybe the Dream Team was better off without me.

Chapter Ten

I was quiet at home that night. It didn't help that my voice sounded far away, talking through a swollen nose.

Mum made a big fuss, clucking around me like a mother hen. Even Ryan, my big brother, fussed over me. He cooked pikelets as an afternoon treat – with extra jam for me.

They thought I was quiet because my nose was hurting.

But that wasn't the reason. My nose didn't feel as bad as the strange, lonely feeling inside.

At bedtime, Mum sat with me singing 'You Are My Sunshine' like she used to when I was little. Soon my whole body seemed to sink into the sheets. Mum's voice was far away as I drifted off to sleep.

I am on the netball court, playing with my friends. I feel light and sporty — like I could fly.

I throw the ball easily. It flies between us. My friends smile and throw it back.

Suddenly, I realise I am in my pyjamas. I look around, embarrassed. It feels like I am sinking, sinking, down into a spongy netball court. I call for the ball, but no-one can hear me. My legs *are stuck and I can't move. It's like I'm under water. Around me, the ball still flies around. Then I see a new face. A stranger is playing with my team! She is tall, strong, sporty. I realise she is someone to help them win the grand final.*

The shock of seeing the new player hits me, hard. In a fog, the court slowly fades into the distance. My team stays in the dream, playing in the grand final without me.

When I woke up, the house was quiet. Everyone was asleep. I felt as if I were the only person awake in the world.

I rolled onto my back. My star and moon stickers glowed on the ceiling. Inside I felt heavy and empty. Not a good feeling. Not a good dream.

I wasn't used to caring about sport like this. Life was better when I didn't have to worry about letting my team down.

I sat up and turned on my light, trying to shake the dream from my mind. *Never mind,* I said to myself. *It's not about winning. It's about joining in and having fun.*

And I had been doing that. I was on a team with friends. But it was no fun being hit in the nose or dropping the ball. It was no fun if I stopped everyone else from winning.

I slumped back on my pillow with the light still on. I thought about Becky, Angie and Claire. I thought about Callum, Mickey and Brad. They were such brilliant friends to me. I really didn't want to let them down … again.

And lying there, in the cold light of the lamp, I realised what I had to do.

It was a strange plan. But maybe it would work.

I couldn't always catch a ball. But here was something I *could* do – a way to help my friends win the grand final.

Chapter Eleven

For the rest of the week, I sat and watched.

No more playing netball for me.

That was part of my plan.

Sitting and watching was harder than I expected. Especially once my nose felt better. But that was a secret. I told everyone I couldn't play because my nose still hurt.

Sometimes I had to sit on my hands and cross my ankles under the bench. Otherwise, if the ball came near, my feet would try to jump up and my hands would try to catch it.

Each time they took a break, Becky would bring me drinks and check how I was doing. But I didn't tell her about my plan.

Angie kept glancing over as me as she played. I'm not sure why. She did it so often that sometimes she even missed the ball.

The third time she did it, Callum called out, 'Angie! Keep your eyes on the BALL.'

She glared at him like she wanted to start yelling.

Normally, I would have called out a joke or tried to cheer them up. They didn't need to fight. But instead I stayed quiet and sat out.

It's all part of my plan!

Then, during lunchtime on the day of the grand final, Angie walked over. 'Come and play,' she said quietly. 'I won't throw hard. Promise.'

I looked down at my knees. I could hear the rest of the team calling to each other as they played. 'I'll see how I feel,' I said.

'We need you, Alex.' Angie's voice had pleading sound to it.

But I just shrugged. Angie would understand once I helped them win the grand final.

I couldn't give up now.

I had made it through the first part of my plan. Now it was time for the second part – my grand-final plan.

'Alex, are you in here?'

It was Becky, looking for me. But I didn't want to be found. I was hiding in the girls' toilets.

That was my grand-final plan.

Once my team couldn't find me, they would have to start playing the grand final without me. Perfect! Without me to mess up, they would win for sure.

But I hadn't counted on Becky finding me before the game.

I was sitting on the lid of the toilet, hugging my legs tight. Becky's shadow moved under the toilet door. I heard puffing as she tried to peer under the door.

'Alex, open the door!' Becky's voice sounded funny from leaning low.

Without making a sound, I reached out and undid the lock. Maybe if I told Becky my plan, then she would help me hide.

But as the door swung open, a surprise awaited me. Becky wasn't alone.

Behind her stood the whole team, even the boys!

I let out a giggle and pointed. 'Hey, you're in the girls' toilets!'

But no-one was laughing. Not even Mickey. Angie's eyes were flashing, like when Callum told her what to do.

Suddenly I felt as if I had been caught doing something wrong. *Was my grand-final plan a bad one?*

Chapter Twelve

Suddenly I was scared. In front of me, crowded into the girls' toilets, stood my favourite friends in the whole school. I didn't want to make them angry!

In my mind I thought about my plan, and about how I always dropped the ball and made mistakes. I knew I could help them by sitting out.

But when I spoke, all that came out was a stammer. 'I'm just … you see … I …'

Becky held my hand. 'Come and play, Alex,' she said kindly.

'Yeah,' said everyone behind her.

I fiddled with the lock, feeling silly and shy. 'But I'll just drop the ball and make you lose.'

That was the truth, after all.

Angie rolled her eyes. 'Alex, we NEED you!'

'No you don't. You —' I wanted to explain that they were better off without me. But I didn't get the chance.

Everyone started talking at once. It was strange. No-one seemed angry about my bad ball skills. They all had good things to say about me.

Everyone seemed to think I did heaps of things to help the team – things that no-one else did.

When everyone had finished talking, I just stared at them, surprised.

'Think about it,' said Becky. 'Who stopped Angie and Callum from fighting at the start?'

'And whose idea was it to make us think of our basketball coach's tactics?' said Callum.

I started to smile.

'And who thought of our name? And made the poster?' asked Claire.

I giggled. 'I've been busy, haven't I?'

Then Mickey spoke up from the back. 'Yeah, and you say those dumb jokes.'

I put my hands on my hips. 'No, I don't!' I smiled. 'My jokes are clever and funny.'

Everyone groaned.

And suddenly, I knew exactly what I had to do.

I had to join the team again, and play in the grand final. We would be a bunch of friends playing netball together. The Dream Team again.

So that's exactly what I did.

At first I felt scared of that nasty gremlin ball. I hadn't played netball since I was hit in the nose. *What if that happened again?*

But I couldn't worry for too long. I didn't have time. Soon I was racing around, sticking to my player like glue.

I'm going to help us win.

We were playing against the best team, the one with the girls who played on a team outside of school. They kept grunting and growling at each other, as if playing the grand final made them angry.

Angie and Callum met them head on. When the other team played rough, they did too.

This was sport at its toughest.

Then, when I was in a gap, Angie threw me the ball. It was a gentle throw, too slow. Someone from the other team jumped up and snatched the ball in a flash.

'Grrr!' growled Angie. She thumped her leg with her fist, angry at herself.

But I didn't want Angie to feel bad.

'Hey Angie!' I called. 'Aim at the bib! Not the person's face.'

For a moment, she looked at me, confused and a bit annoyed. Our eyes met and I smiled cheekily.

Then Angie smiled. Suddenly she realised what I was doing. *The worst player telling the best player what to do?* How silly!

That was pretty funny!

But it worked.

Angie relaxed after that. The whole team did. We started calling more, and laughing at ourselves even when things went wrong.

When it was all over, I felt light and happy and proud. Not because of the score, but because I had found my place in the team again.

We lost the grand final by seven goals. But we had done it together, and I had helped the team.

That game was my favourite of all.

Chapter Thirteen

I leant out a plucked a blade of grass. Then I split it in half with my thumbnail.

It was the last day of P.E. for the term. We sat on the oval while Mr Dwyer explained the rules of tunnel ball.

But I was only half-listening. No more netball. And no more Dream Team! I felt a bit sad.

In a dream, I pulled at another blade of grass. But Becky shook my arm.

'Alex!' she said, pointing to Mr Dwyer.

Mr Dwyer was looking at me with raised eyebrows. 'Awesome Alex!' he said. 'You're one of the tunnel ball captains.'

I gulped and stood up. *Me, a captain?* This was something new. For once I didn't have to worry about being last person picked.

The other captains started choosing their teams. I scanned the faces in front of me. *Who should I choose?*

Of course, I started with everyone on the Dream Team. Just to make him squirm, I left Callum until last. When I called his name, he wiped his forehead and said,

'Phew!' in a jokey way.

But I still had three more choices. *Who next?* Lots of faces looked up at me. Some kids were sitting straight and hopeful. Others were staring at the ground, looking bored. One boy was scratching a mozzie bite on his arm.

Then I saw another face. He was sitting up the back, ready to wait until the end.

'Tony!' I called out.

Slowly, Tony stood up. He looked surprised to have been chosen so soon. As Tony walked over to us, I glanced back at the gang. Would they be upset that I chose someone so bad at sport?

But Brad and the girls were smiling.

Mickey was giving Tony the thumbs-up. Best of all, Tony was beaming.

'I'm not so bad at tunnel ball,' he said, grinning.

And he was right. Tony actually wasn't the worst on our team. To my surprise, Callum was!

In tunnel ball, the team stands in a long line and forms a tunnel. Everyone has to lean down and push the ball through their legs.

But Callum's really tall. He had trouble folding his long body and reaching way down to the ground. His big feet kept getting in the way, too.

At one point Callum lost his balance

and fell backwards onto Mickey. As they fell, they pushed everyone behind them over, like dominoes.

'Argh!' Poor Becky was squished at the end.

'Up you get!' called Mr Dwyer.

But everyone had the giggles. Claire was laughing so much that she fell down and knocked us over again. I think she did it on purpose.

It was pretty silly, but loads of fun.

By now, the other teams had finished and were shaking their heads at us – a laughing, groaning line of bodies.

We had no chance of winning now! I rolled out from under Angie and stood in front of my team. 'Right! Good warm-up, everyone,' I called. 'Now let's play the game.'

My team stood up straight, with beaming faces and weak giggly legs.

Mr Dwyer smiled at me and winked. He seemed proud of me as captain.

I smiled back. I was proud of myself. And I was proud of my team, too.

Collect them all!

Sleep-over

Boy-friend?

Surf's Up

Flower Girl

Dancing Queen

Camp Chaos

Sister Spirit

Back to School

Sink or Swim

Birthday Girl

The Worst Gymnast

Music Mad

Best Christmas Ever

Class Captain

The New Girl

Karate Kicks

Secret's Out

Holiday!

Netball Dreams

The Big Split

www.gogirlhq.com